William Butler Yeats

Two Plays for Dancers

Outlook

William Butler Yeats

Two Plays for Dancers

1. Auflage | ISBN: 978-3-73261-864-4

Erscheinungsort: Paderborn, Deutschland

Erscheinungsjahr: 2018

Outlook Verlag GmbH, Paderborn.

William Butler Yeats

Two Plays for Dancers

Outlook

TWO PLAYS FOR DANCERS

BY W. B. YEATS

THE CUALA PRESS
MCMXIX

TWO PLAYS FOR DANCERS

PREFACE

In a note at the end of my last book 'The Wild Swans at Coole' (Cuala Press.) I explained why I preferred this kind of drama, and where I had found my models, and where and how my first play after this kind was performed, and when and how I would have it performed in the future. I can but refer the reader to the note or to the long introduction to 'Certain Noble Plays of Japan' (Cuala Press.)

W. B. Yeats. October 11th. 1918

P. S. That I might write 'The Dreaming of the Bones,' Mr. W. A. Henderson with great kindness wrote out for me all historical allusions to Dervorgilla.

THE DREAMING OF THE BONES

The stage is any bare place in a room close to the wall. A screen with a pattern of mountain and sky can stand against the wall, or a curtain with a like pattern hang upon it, but the pattern must only symbolize or suggest. One musician enters and then two others, the first stands singing while the others take their places. Then all three sit down against the wall by their instruments, which are already there—a drum, a zither, and a flute. Or they unfold a cloth as in 'The Hawk's Well,' while the instruments are carried in.

FIRST MUSICIAN

(or all three musicians, singing)
Why does my heart beat so?
Did not a shadow pass?
It passed but a moment ago.
Who can have trod in the grass?
What rogue is night-wandering?
Have not old writers said
That dizzy dreams can spring
From the dry bones of the dead?
And many a night it seems
That all the valley fills
With those fantastic dreams.
They overflow the hills,
So passionate is a shade,
Like wine that fills to the top
A grey-green cup of jade,
Or maybe an agate cup.
(speaking) The hour before dawn and the moon covered up.
The little village of Abbey is covered up;
The little narrow trodden way that runs
From the white road to the Abbey of Corcomroe
Is covered up; and all about the hills
Are like a circle of Agate or of Jade.
Somewhere among great rocks on the scarce grass
Birds cry, they cry their loneliness.
Even the sunlight can be lonely here,
Even hot noon is lonely. I hear a footfall—
A young man with a lantern comes this way.

He seems an Aran fisher, for he wears
The flannel bawneen and the cow-hide shoe.
He stumbles wearily, and stumbling prays.

(A young man enters, praying in Irish)

Once more the birds cry in their loneliness,
But now they wheel about our heads; and now
They have dropped on the grey stone to the north-east.

(A man and a girl both in the costume of a past time, come in.
They wear heroic masks)

YOUNG MAN

(raising his lantern)
Who is there? I cannot see what you are like,
Come to the light.

STRANGER

But what have you to fear?

YOUNG MAN

And why have you come creeping through the dark.

(The Girl blows out lantern)

The wind has blown my lantern out. Where are you?
I saw a pair of heads against the sky
And lost them after, but you are in the right
I should not be afraid in County Clare;
And should be or should not be have no choice,
I have to put myself into your hands,
Now that my candle's out.

STRANGER

You have fought in Dublin?

YOUNG MAN

I was in the Post Office, and if taken
I shall be put against a wall and shot.

STRANGER

You know some place of refuge, have some plan
Or friend who will come to meet you?

YOUNG MAN

                              I am to lie
At daybreak on the mountain and keep watch
Until an Aran coracle puts in
At Muckanish or at the rocky shore
Under Finvarra, but would break my neck
If I went stumbling there alone in the dark.

STRANGER

We know the pathways that the sheep tread out,
And all the hiding-places of the hills,
And that they had better hiding-places once.

YOUNG MAN

You'd say they had better before English robbers
Cut down the trees or set them upon fire
For fear their owners might find shelter there.
What is that sound?

STRANGER

                              An old horse gone astray
He has been wandering on the road all night.

YOUNG MAN

I took him for a man and horse. Police
Are out upon the roads. In the late Rising
I think there was no man of us but hated

To fire at soldiers who but did their duty
And were not of our race, but when a man
Is born in Ireland and of Irish stock
When he takes part against us—

STRANGER

I will put you safe,
No living man shall set his eyes upon you.
I will not answer for the dead.

YOUNG MAN

The dead?

STRANGER

For certain days the stones where you must lie
Have in the hour before the break of day
Been haunted.

YOUNG MAN

But I was not born at midnight.

STRANGER

Many a man born in the full daylight
Can see them plain, will pass them on the high-road
Or in the crowded market-place of the town,
And never know that they have passed.

YOUNG MAN

My Grandam
Would have it they did penance everywhere
Or lived through their old lives again.

STRANGER

In a dream;

And some for an old scruple must hang spitted
Upon the swaying tops of lofty trees;
Some are consumed in fire, some withered up
By hail and sleet out of the wintry North,
And some but live through their old lives again.

YOUNG MAN

Well, let them dream into what shape they please
And fill waste mountains with the invisible tumult
Of the fantastic conscience. I have no dread;
They cannot put me into jail or shoot me,
And seeing that their blood has returned to fields
That have grown red from drinking blood like mine
They would not if they could betray.

STRANGER

This pathway

Runs to the ruined Abbey of Corcomroe;
The Abbey passed, we are soon among the stone
And shall be at the ridge before the cocks
Of Aughanish or Bailevlehan
Or grey Aughtmana shake their wings and cry.

(They go round the stage once)

FIRST MUSICIAN

(speaking) They've passed the shallow well and the flat stone
Fouled by the drinking cattle, the narrow lane
Where mourners for five centuries have carried
Noble or peasant to his burial.
An owl is crying out above their heads.
(singing) Why should the heart take fright
What sets it beating so?
The bitter sweetness of the night
Has made it but a lonely thing.
Red bird of March, begin to crow,
Up with the neck and clap the wing,

Red cock, and crow.

(They go once round the stage. The first musician speaks.)

And now they have climbed through the long grassy field
And passed the ragged thorn trees and the gap
In the ancient hedge; and the tomb-nested owl
At the foot's level beats with a vague wing.
(singing) My head is in a cloud;
I'd let the whole world go.
My rascal heart is proud
Remembering and remembering.
Red bird of March, begin to crow,
Up with the neck and clap the wing
Red cock and crow.

(They go round the stage. The first musician speaks.)

They are among the stones above the ash
Above the briar and thorn and the scarce grass;
Hidden amid the shadow far below them
The cat-headed bird is crying out.
(singing) The dreaming bones cry out
Because the night winds blow
And heaven's a cloudy blot;
Calamity can have its fling.
Red bird of March begin to crow,
Up with the neck and clap the wing
Red cock and crow.

THE STRANGER

We're almost at the summit and can rest.
The road is a faint shadow there; and there
The abbey lies amid its broken tombs.
In the old days we should have heard a bell
Calling the monks before day broke to pray;
And when the day has broken on the ridge,
The crowing of its cocks.

YOUNG MAN

Is there no house

Famous for sanctity or architectural beauty
In Clare or Kerry, or in all wide Connacht
The enemy has not unroofed?

STRANGER

Close to the altar
Broken by wind and frost and worn by time
Donogh O'Brien has a tomb, a name in Latin.
He wore fine clothes and knew the secrets of women
But he rebelled against the King of Thomond
And died in his youth.

YOUNG MAN

And why should he rebel?
The King of Thomond was his rightful master.
It was men like Donogh who made Ireland weak—
My curse on all that troop, and when I die
I'll leave my body, if I have any choice,
Far from his ivy tod and his owl; have those
Who, if your tale is true, work out a penance
Upon the mountain-top where I am to hide,
Come from the Abbey graveyard?

THE GIRL

They have not that luck,
But are more lonely, those that are buried there,
Warred in the heat of the blood; if they were rebels
Some momentary impulse made them rebels
Or the comandment of some petty king
Who hated Thomond. Being but common sinners,
No callers in of the alien from oversea
They and their enemies of Thomond's party
Mix in a brief dream battle above their bones,
Or make one drove or drift in amity,
Or in the hurry of the heavenly round
Forget their earthly names; these are alone
Being accursed.

YOUNG MAN

And if what seems is true
And there are more upon the other side
Than on this side of death, many a ghost
Must meet them face to face and pass the word
Even upon this grey and desolate hill.

YOUNG GIRL

Until this hour no ghost or living man
Has spoken though seven centuries have run
Since they, weary of life and of men's eyes,
Flung down their bones in some forgotten place
Being accursed.

YOUNG MAN

I have heard that there are souls
Who, having sinned after a monstrous fashion
Take on them, being dead, a monstrous image
To drive the living, should they meet its face,
Crazy, and be a terror to the dead.

YOUNG GIRL

But these
Were comely even in their middle life
And carry, now that they are dead, the image
Of their first youth, for it was in that youth
Their sin began.

YOUNG MAN

I have heard of angry ghosts
Who wander in a wilful solitude.

THE GIRL

These have no thought but love; nor joy

But that upon the instant when their penance
Draws to its height and when two hearts are wrung
Nearest to breaking, if hearts of shadows break,
His eyes can mix with hers; nor any pang
That is so bitter as that double glance,
Being accursed.

YOUNG MAN

But what is this strange penance—
That when their eyes have met can wring them most?

THE GIRL

Though eyes can meet, their lips can never meet.

YOUNG MAN

And yet it seems they wander side by side.
But doubtless you would say that when lips meet
And have not living nerves, it is no meeting.

THE GIRL

Although they have no blood or living nerves
Who once lay warm and live the live-long night
In one another's arms, and know their part
In life, being now but of the people of dreams,
Is a dreams part; although they are but shadows
Hovering between a thorn tree and a stone
Who have heaped up night on winged night; although
No shade however harried and consumed
Would change his own calamity for theirs,
Their manner of life were blessed could their lips
A moment meet; but when he has bent his head
Close to her head or hand would slip in hand
The memory of their crime flows up between
And drives them apart.

YOUNG MAN

                                    The memory of a crime—
He took her from a husband's house it may be,
But does the penance for a passionate sin
Last for so many centuries?

THE GIRL

                                                    No, no,
The man she chose, the man she was chosen by
Cared little and cares little from whose house
They fled towards dawn amid the flights of arrows
Or that it was a husband's and a king's;
And how if that were all could she lack friends
On crowded roads or on the unpeopled hill?
Helen herself had opened wide the door
Where night by night she dreams herself awake
And gathers to her breast a dreaming man.

YOUNG MAN

What crime can stay so in the memory?
What crime can keep apart the lips of lovers
Wandering and alone?

THE GIRL

                                        Her king and lover
Was overthrown in battle by her husband
And for her sake and for his own, being blind
And bitter and bitterly in love, he brought
A foreign army from across the sea.

YOUNG MAN

You speak of Dermot and of Dervorgilla
Who brought the Norman in?

THE GIRL

                                        Yes, yes I spoke

Of that most miserable, most accursed pair
Who sold their country into slavery, and yet
They were not wholly miserable and accursed
If somebody of their race at last would say:
'I have forgiven them.'

YOUNG MAN

Oh, never, never
Will Dermot and Dervorgilla be forgiven.

THE GIRL

If someone of their race forgave at last
Lip would be pressed on lip.

YOUNG MAN

Oh, never, never
Will Dermot and Dervorgilla be forgiven.
You have told your story well, so well indeed
I could not help but fall into the mood
And for a while believe that it was true
Or half believe, but better push on now.
The horizon to the East is growing bright.

(They go once round stage)

So here we're on the summit. I can see
The Aran Islands, Connemara Hills,
And Galway in the breaking light; there too
The enemy has toppled wall and roof
And torn from ancient walls to boil his pot
The oaken panelling that had been dear
To generations of children and old men.
But for that pair for whom you would have my pardon
It might be now like Bayeux or like Caen
Or little Italian town amid its walls
For though we have neither coal nor iron ore
To make us rich and cover heaven with smoke
Our country, if that crime were uncommitted
Had been most beautiful. Why do you dance?

Why do you gaze and with so passionate eyes
One on the other and then turn away
Covering your eyes and weave it in a dance,
Who are you? what are you? you are not natural.

THE GIRL

Seven hundred years our lips have never met.

YOUNG MAN

Why do you look so strangely at one another,
So strangely and so sweetly?

THE GIRL

Seven hundred years.

YOUNG MAN

So strangely and so sweetly. All the ruin,
All, all their handiwork is blown away
As though the mountain air had blown it away
Because their eyes have met. They cannot hear,
Being folded up and hidden in their dance.
The dance is changing now. They have dropped their eyes,
They have covered up their eyes as though their hearts
Had suddenly been broken—never, never
Shall Dermot and Dervorgilla be forgiven.
They have drifted in the dance from rock to rock.
They have raised their hands as though to snatch the sleep
That lingers always in the abyss of the sky
Though they can never reach it. A cloud floats up
And covers all the mountain head in a moment.
And now it lifts and they are swept away.
I had almost yielded and forgiven it all—
This is indeed a place of terrible temptation.

> (The Musicians begin unfolding and folding a black cloth. The
> First Musician comes forward to the front of the stage, at the
> centre. He holds the cloth before him. The other two come one on

either side and unfold it. They afterwards fold it up in the same
way. While it is unfolded, the Young Man leaves the stage)

THE MUSICIANS

I

(singing) At the grey round of the hill
Music of a lost kingdom
Runs, runs and is suddenly still.
The winds out of Clare-Galway
Carry it: suddenly it is still.

I have heard in the night air
A wandering airy music;
And moidered in that snare
A man is lost of a sudden,
In that sweet wandering snare.

What finger first began
Music of a lost kingdom.
They dreamed that laughed in the sun.
Dry bones that dream are bitter,
They dream and darken our sun.

Those crazy fingers play
A wandering airy music;
Our luck is withered away,
And wheat in the wheat-ear withered,
And the wind blows it away.

II

My heart ran wild when it heard
The curlew cry before dawn
And the eddying cat-headed bird;
But now the night is gone.
I have heard from far below
The strong March birds a-crow,
Stretch neck and clap the wing,
Red cocks, and crow.

THE ONLY JEALOUSY OF EMER

Enter Musicians, who are dressed as in the earlier play. They have the same musical instruments, which can either be already upon the stage or be brought in by the First Musician before he stands in the centre with the cloth between his hands, or by a player when the cloth is unfolded. The stage as before can be against the wall of any room.

FIRST MUSICIAN

(During the unfolding and folding of the cloth)

A woman's beauty is like a white
Frail bird, like a white sea-bird alone
At daybreak after stormy night
Between two furrows upon the ploughed land:
A sudden storm and it was thrown
Between dark furrows upon the ploughed land.
How many centuries spent
The sedentary soul
In toils of measurement
Beyond eagle or mole,
Beyond hearing or seeing,
Or Archimedes guess,
To raise into being
That loveliness?

A strange unserviceable thing,
A fragile, exquisite, pale shell,
That the vast troubled waters bring
To the loud sands before day has broken.
The storm arose and suddenly fell
Amid the dark before day had broken.
What death? what discipline?
What bonds no man could unbind
Being imagined within
The labyrinth of the mind?
What pursuing or fleeing?
What wounds, what bloody press?
Dragged into being
This loveliness.

(When the cloth is folded again the Musicians take their place against wall. The folding of the cloth shows on one side of the stage the curtained bed or litter on which lies a man in his grave- clothes. He wears an heroic mask. Another man with exactly similar clothes and mask crouches near the front. Emer is sitting beside the bed.)

FIRST MUSICIAN

(speaking) I call before the eyes a roof
With cross-beams darkened by smoke.
A fisher's net hangs from a beam,
A long oar lies against the wall.
I call up a poor fisher's house.
A man lies dead or swooning,
That amorous man,
That amorous, violent man, renowned Cuchulain,
Queen Emer at his side.
At her own bidding all the rest have gone.
But now one comes on hesitating feet,
Young Eithne Inguba, Cuchulain's mistress.
She stands a moment in the open door,
Beyond the open door the bitter sea,
The shining, bitter sea is crying out,
(singing) White shell, white wing
I will not choose for my friend
A frail unserviceable thing
That drifts and dreams, and but knows
That waters are without end
And that wind blows.

EMER

(speaking) Come hither, come sit down beside the bed
You need not be afraid, for I myself
Sent for you, Eithne Inguba.

EITHNE INGUBA

No, Madam,
I have too deeply wronged you to sit there.

EMER

Of all the people in the world we two,
And we alone, may watch togetherhere,
Because we have loved him best.

EITHNE INGUBA

And is he dead?

EMER

Although they have dressed him out in his grave-clothes
And stretched his limbs, Cuchulain is not dead;
The very heavens when that day's at hand,
So that his death may not lack ceremony,
Will throw out fires, and the earth grow red with blood.
There shall not be a scullion but foreknows it
Like the world's end.

EITHNE INGUBA

How did he come to this?

EMER

Towards noon in the assembly of the kings
He met with one who seemed a while most dear.
The kings stood round; some quarrel was blown up;
He drove him out and killed him on the shore
At Baile's tree, and he who was so killed
Was his own son begot on some wild woman
When he was young, or so I have heard it said;
And thereupon, knowing what man he had killed,
And being mad with sorrow, he ran out;
And after to his middle in the foam
With shield before him and with sword in hand,
He fought the deathless sea. The kings looked on
And not a king dared stretch an arm, or even
Dared call his name, but all stood wondering

In that dumb stupor like cattle in a gale,
Until at last, as though he had fixed his eyes
On a new enemy, he waded out
Until the water had swept over him;
But the waves washed his senseless image up
And laid it at this door.

EITHNE INGUBA

How pale he looks!

EMER

He is not dead.

EITHNE INGUBA

You have not kissed his lips
Nor laid his head upon your breast.

EMER

It may be
An image has been put into his place,
A sea-born log bewitched into his likeness,
Or some stark horseman grown too old to ride
Among the troops of Mananan, Son of the Sea,
Now that his joints are stiff.

EITHNE INGUBA

Cry out his name.
All that are taken from our sight, they say,
Loiter amid the scenery of their lives
For certain hours or days, and should he hear
He might, being angry drive the changeling out.

EMER

It is hard to make them hear amid their darkness,

And it is long since I could call him home;
I am but his wife, but if you cry aloud
With that sweet voice that is so dear to him
He cannot help but listen.

EITHNE INGUBA

He loves me best,
Being his newest love, but in the end
Will love the woman best who loved him first
And loved him through the years when love seemed lost.

EMER

I have that hope, the hope that some day and somewhere
We'll sit together at the hearth again.

EITHNE INGUBA

Women like me when the violent hour is over
Are flung into some corner like old nut shells.
Cuchulain, listen.

EMER

No, not yet for first
I'll cover up his face to hide the sea;
And throw new logs upon the hearth and stir
The half burnt logs until they break in flame.
Old Mananan's unbridled horses come
Out of the sea and on their backs his horsemen
But all the enchantments of the dreaming foam
Dread the hearth fire.

> (She pulls the curtains of the bed so as to hide the sick man's face,
> that the actor may change his mask unseen. She goes to one side
> of platform and moves her hand as though putting logs on a fire
> and stirring it into a blaze. While she makes these movements the
> Musicians play, marking the movements with drum and flute
> perhaps.
>
> Having finished she stands beside the imaginary fire at a distance

from Cuchulain & Eithne Inguba.)

Call on Cuchulain now.

EITHNE INGUBA

Can you not hear my voice.

EMER

Bend over him.
Call out dear secrets till you have touched his heart
If he lies there; and if he is not there
Till you have made him jealous.

EITHNE INGUBA

Cuchulain, listen.

EMER

You speak too timidly; to be afraid
Because his wife is but three paces off
When there is so great a need were but to prove
The man that chose you made but a poor choice.
We're but two women struggling with the sea.

EITHNE INGUBA

O my beloved pardon me, that I
Have been ashamed and you in so great need.
I have never sent a message or called out,
Scarce had a longing for your company
But you have known and come; and if indeed
You are lying there stretch out your arms and speak;
Open your mouth and speak for to this hour
My company has made you talkative.
Why do you mope, and what has closed your ears.
Our passion had not chilled when we were parted
On the pale shore under the breaking dawn.
He will not hear me: or his ears are closed
And no sound reaches him.

EMER

Then kiss that image
The pressure of your mouth upon his mouth
May reach him where he is.

EITHNE INGUBA

(starting back) It is no man.
I felt some evil thing that dried my heart
When my lips touched it.

EMER

No, his body stirs;
The pressure of your mouth has called him home;
He has thrown the changeling out.

EITHNE INGUBA

(going further off) Look at that arm
That arm is withered to the very socket.

EMER

(going up to the bed)
What do you come for and from where?

FIGURE of CUCHULAIN

I have come
From Mananan's court upon a bridleless horse.

EMER

What one among the Sidhe has dared to lie
Upon Cuchulain's bed and take his image?

FIGURE of CUCHULAIN

I am named Bricriu—not the man—that Bricriu,
Maker of discord among gods and men,
Called Bricriu of the Sidhe.

EMER

Come for what purpose?

FIGURE of CUCHULAIN

(sitting up and showing its distorted face. Eithne Inguba goes out)

I show my face and everything he loves
Must fly away.

EMER

You people of the wind
Are full of lying speech and mockery.
I have not fled your face.

FIGURE of CUCHULAIN

You are not loved.

EMER

And therefore have no dread to meet your eyes
And to demand him of you.

FIGURE of CUCHULAIN

For that I have come.
You have but to pay the price and he is free.

EMER

Do the Sidhe bargain?

FIGURE of CUCHULAIN

When they set free a captive
They take in ransom a less valued thing.
The fisher when some knowledgeable man
Restores to him his wife, or son, or daughter,
Knows he must lose a boat or net, or it may be
The cow that gives his children milk; and some
Have offered their own lives. I do not ask

Your life, or any valuable thing;
You spoke but now of the mere chance that some day
You'd sit together by the hearth again;
Renounce that chance, that miserable hour,
And he shall live again.

EMER

                                        I do not question
But you have brought ill luck on all he loves
And now, because I am thrown beyond your power
Unless your words are lies, you come to bargain.

FIGURE of CUCHULAIN

You loved your power when but newly married
And I love mine although I am old and withered;
You have but to put yourself into that power And
he shall live again.

EMER

                                        No, never, never.

FIGURE of CUCHULAIN

You dare not be accursed yet he has dared.

EMER

I have but two joyous thoughts, two things I prize,
A hope, a memory, and now you claim that hope.

FIGURE of CUCHULAIN

He'll never sit beside you at the hearth
Or make old bones, but die of wounds and toil
On some far shore or mountain, a strange woman
Beside his mattress.

EMER

You ask for my one hope
That you may bring your curse on all about him.

FIGURE of CUCHULAIN

You've watched his loves and you have not been jealous
Knowing that he would tire, but do those tire
That love the Sidhe?

EMER

What dancer of the Sidhe
What creature of the reeling moon has pursued him?

FIGURE of CUCHULAIN

I have but to touch your eyes and give them sight;
But stand at my left side.

(He touches her eyes with his left hand, the right being withered)

EMER

My husband there.

FIGURE of CUCHULAIN

But out of reach—I have dissolved the dark
That hid him from your eyes but not that other
That's hidden you from his.

EMER

Husband, husband!

FIGURE of CUCHULAIN

Be silent, he is but a phantom now

And he can neither touch, nor hear, nor see;
The longing and the cries have drawn him hither.
He heard no sound, heard no articulate sound;
They could but banish rest, and make him dream,
And in that dream, as do all dreaming shades
Before they are accustomed to their freedom,
He has taken his familiar form, and yet
He crouches there not knowing where he is
Or at whose side he is crouched.

> (a Woman of the Sidhe has entered and stands a little inside the door)

EMER

Who is this woman?

FIGURE of CUCHULAIN

She has hurried from the Country-Under-Wave
And dreamed herself into that shape that he
May glitter in her basket; for the Sidhe
Are fishers also and they fish for men
With dreams upon the hook.

EMER

And so that woman
Has hid herself in this disguise and made
Herself into a lie.

FIGURE of CUCHULAIN

A dream is body;
The dead move ever towards a dreamless youth
And when they dream no more return no more;
And those more holy shades that never lived
But visit you in dreams.

EMER

                                              I know her sort.
They find our men asleep, weary with war,
Or weary with the chase and kiss their lips
And drop their hair upon them, from that hour
Our men, who yet knew nothing of it all,
Are lonely, and when at fall of night we press
Their hearts upon our hearts their hearts are cold.

        (She draws a knife from her girdle)

FIGURE of CUCHULAIN

And so you think to wound her with a knife.
She has an airy body. Look and listen;
I have not given you eyes and ears for nothing.

        (The Woman of the Sidhe moves round the crouching Ghost of
        Cuchulain at front of stage in a dance that grows gradually
        quicker, as he slowly awakes. At moments she may drop her hair
        upon his head but she does not kiss him. She is accompanied by
        string and flute and drum. Her mask and clothes must suggest
        gold or bronze or brass or silver so that she seems more an idol
        than a human being. This suggestion may be repeated in her
        movements. Her hair too, must keep the metallic suggestion.)

GHOST of CUCHULAIN

Who is it stands before me there
Shedding such light from limb and hair
As when the moon complete at last
With every labouring crescent past,
And lonely with extreme delight,
Flings out upon the fifteenth night?

WOMAN of the SIDHE

Because I long I am not complete.
What pulled your hands about your feet
And your head down upon your knees,
And hid your face?

GHOST of CUCHULAIN

                    Old memories:
A dying boy, with handsome face
Upturned upon a beaten place;
A sacred yew-tree on a strand;
A woman that held in steady hand
In all the happiness of her youth
Before her man had broken troth,
A burning wisp to light the door;
And many a round or crescent more;
Dead men and women. Memories
Have pulled my head upon my knees.

WOMAN of the SIDHE

Could you that have loved many a woman
That did not reach beyond the human,
Lacking a day to be complete,
Love one that though her heart can beat,
Lacks it but by an hour or so.

GHOST of CUCHULAIN

I know you now for long ago
I met you on the mountain side,
Beside a well that seemed long dry,
Beside old thorns where the hawk flew.
I held out arms and hands but you,
That now seem friendly, fled away
Half woman and half bird of prey.

WOMAN of the SIDHE

Hold out your arms and hands again
You were not so dumbfounded when
I was that bird of prey and yet
I am all woman now.

GHOST of CUCHULAIN

                              I am not

The young and passionate man I was
And though that brilliant light surpass
All crescent forms, my memories
Weigh down my hands, abash my eyes.

WOMAN of the SIDHE

Then kiss my mouth. Though memory
Be beauty's bitterest enemy
I have no dread for at my kiss
Memory on the moment vanishes:
Nothing but beauty can remain.

GHOST of CUCHULAIN

And shall I never know again
Intricacies of blind remorse?

WOMAN of the SIDHE

Time shall seem to stay his course,
For when your mouth and my mouth meet
All my round shall be complete Imagining
all its circles run;
And there shall be oblivion
Even to quench Cuchulain's drouth,
Even to still that heart.

GHOST of CUCHULAIN

                              Your mouth.

    (They are about to kiss, he turns away)
O Emer, Emer.

WOMAN of the SIDHE

                          So then it is she
Made you impure with memory.

GHOST of CUCHULAIN

Still in that dream I see you stand,
A burning wisp in your right hand,
To wait my coming to the house,
As when our parents married us.

WOMAN of the SIDHE

Being among the dead you love her
That valued every slut above her
While you still lived.

GHOST of CUCHULAIN

O my lost Emer.

WOMAN of the SIDHE

And there is not a loose-tongued schemer
But could draw you if not dead,
From her table and her bed.
How could you be fit to wive
With flesh and blood, being born to live
Where no one speaks of broken troth
For all have washed out of their eyes
Wind blown dirt of their memories
To improve their sight?

GHOST of CUCHULAIN

Your mouth, your mouth.

(Their lips approach but Cuchulain turns away as Emer speaks.)

EMER

If he may live I am content,
Content that he shall turn on me,
If but the dead will set him free
That I may speak with him at whiles,

Eyes that the cold moon or the harsh sea
Or what I know not's made indifferent.

GHOST of CUCHULAIN

What a wise silence has fallen in this dark!
I know you now in all your ignorance
Of all whereby a lover's quiet is rent.
What dread so great as that he should forget
The least chance sight or sound, or scratch or mark
On an old door, or frail bird heard and seen
In the incredible clear light love cast
All round about her some forlorn lost day?
That face, though fine enough, is a fool's face
And there's a folly in the deathless Sidhe
Beyond man's reach.

WOMAN of the SIDHE

I told you to forget
After my fashion; you would have none of it;
So now you may forget in a man's fashion.
There's an unbridled horse at the sea's edge.
Mount; it will carry you in an eye's wink
To where the King of Country-Under-Wave,
Old Mananan, nods above the board and moves
His chessmen in a dream. Demand your life
And come again on the unbridled horse.

GHOST of CUCHULAIN

Forgive me those rough words. How could you know
That man is held to those whom he has loved
By pain they gave, or pain that he has given,
Intricacies of pain.

WOMAN of the SIDHE

I am ashamed
That being of the deathless shades I chose

32

A man so knotted to impurity.

    (The Ghost of Cuchulain goes out)

WOMAN of the SIDHE (to Figure of Cuchulain)

To you that have no living light, but dropped
From a last leprous crescent of the moon,
I owe it all.

FIGURE of CUCHULAIN

                          Because you have failed
I must forego your thanks, I that took pity
Upon your love and carried out your plan
To tangle all his life and make it nothing
That he might turn to you.

WOMAN of the SIDHE

                          Was it from pity
You taught the woman to prevail against me?

FIGURE of CUCHULAIN

You know my nature—by what name I am called.

WOMAN of the SIDHE

Was it from pity that you hid the truth
That men are bound to women by the wrongs
They do or suffer?

FIGURE of CUCHULAIN

                You know what being I am.

WOMAN of the SIDHE

I have been mocked and disobeyed—your power

Was more to you than my good-will, and now
I'll have you learn what my ill-will can do;
I lay you under bonds upon the instant
To stand before our King and face the charge
And take the punishment.

FIGURE of CUCHULAIN

I'll stand there first.
And tell my story first, and Mananan
Knows that his own harsh sea made my heart cold.

WOMAN of the SIDHE

My horse is there and shall outrun your horse.

(The Figure of Cuchulain falls back, the Woman of the Sidhe goes
out. Drum taps, music resembling horse hoofs.)

EITHNE INGUBA (entering quickly)

I heard the beat of hoofs, but saw no horse,
And then came other hoofs and after that
I heard low angry cries and thereupon
I ceased to be afraid.

EMER

Cuchulain wakes.

(The figure turns round. It once more wears the heroic mask.)

CUCHULAIN

Eithne Inguba take me in your arms,
I have been in some strange place and am afraid.

(The First Musician comes to the front of stage, the others from
each side and unfold the cloth singing)

THE MUSICIANS

What makes her heart beat thus,
Plain to be understood
I have met in a man's house
A statue of solitude,
Moving there and walking;
Its strange heart beating fast
For all our talking.
O still that heart at last.

O bitter reward!
Of many a tragic tomb!
And we though astonished are dumb
And give but a sigh and a word
A passing word.

Although the door be shut
And all seem well enough,
Although wide world hold not
A man but will give you his love.
The moment he has looked at you,
He that has loved the best
May turn from a statue
His too human breast.

O bitter reward!
Of many a tragic tomb!
And we though astonished are dumb
Or give but a sigh and a word
A passing word.

What makes your heart so beat?
Some one should stay at her side.
When beauty is complete
Her own thought will have died
And danger not be diminished;
Dimmed at three quarter light
When moon's round is finished
The stars are out of sight.

O bitter reward!
Of many a tragic tomb!
And we though astonished are dumb
Or give but a sigh and a word
A passing word.

(When the cloth is folded again the stage is bare.)

Here ends, 'Two Plays for Dancers,' by William Butler Yeats. Four hundred copies of this book have been printed and published by Elizabeth Corbet Yeats on paper made in Ireland, at the Cuala Press, Churchtown, Dundrum, in the County of Dublin, Ireland. Finished on the tenth day of January in the year nineteen hundred and nineteen.

www.ingramcontent.com/pod-product-compliance
Lightning Source LLC
Chambersburg PA
CBHW032347020726
47499CB00009B/3203

Xenophon

On Horsemanship

1. Auflage | ISBN: 978-3-73262-089-0

Erscheinungsort: Frankfurt am Main, Deutschland

Erscheinungsjahr: 2018

Outlook Verlag GmbH, Frankfurt.

Xenophon

On Horsemanship

Outlook

ON HORSEMANSHIP

By Xenophon

Translation by H. G. Dakyns

Xenophon the Athenian was born 431 B.C. He was a
pupil of Socrates. He marched with the Spartans,
and was exiled from Athens. Sparta gave him land
and property in Scillus, where he lived for many
years before having to move once more, to settle
in Corinth. He died in 354 B.C.

On Horsemanship advises the reader on how to buy
a good horse, and how to raise it to be either a
war horse or show horse. Xenophon ends with some
words on military equipment for a cavalryman.

Contents

ON HORSEMANSHIP

I

Claiming to have attained some proficiency in horsemanship (1) ourselves, as the result of long experience in the field, our wish is to explain, for the benefit of our younger friends, what we conceive to be the most correct method of dealing with horses.

(1) Lit. "Since, through the accident of having for a long time 'ridden' ourselves, we believe we have become proficients in horsemanship, we wish to show to our younger friends how, as we conceive the matter, they will proceed most correctly in dealing with horses." {ippeuein} in the case of Xenophon = serve as a {ippeus}, whether technically as an Athenian "knight" or more particularly in reference to his organisation of a troop of cavalry during "the retreat" ("Anab." III. iii. 8-20), and, as is commonly believed, while serving under Agesilaus ("Hell." III. iv. 14) in Asia, 396, 395 B.C.

There is, it is true, a treatise on horsemanship written by Simon, the same who dedicated the bronze horse near the Eleusinion in Athens (2) with a representation of his exploits engraved in relief on the pedestal. (3) But we shall not on that account expunge from our treatise any conclusions in which we happen to agree with that author; on the contrary we shall hand them on with still greater pleasure to our friends, in the belief that we shall only gain in authority from the fact that so great an expert in horsemanship held similar views to our own; whilst with regard to matters omitted in his treatise, we shall endeavour to supply them.

(2) L. Dind. (in Athens). The Eleusinion. For the position of this sanctuary of Demeter and Kore see Leake, "Top. of Athens," i. p. 296 foll. For Simon see Sauppe, vol. v. Praef. to "de R. E." p. 230; L. Dind. Praef. "Xen. Opusc." p. xx.; Dr. Morris H. Morgan, "The Art of Horsemanship by Xenophon," p. 119 foll. A fragment of the work referred to, {peri eidous kai ekloges ippon}, exists. The MS. is in the library of Emmanual Coll. Cant. It so happens that one of the hipparchs (?) appealed to by Demosthenes in Arist. "Knights," 242.

{andres ippes, paragenesthe nun o kairos, o Simon, o Panaiti, ouk elate pros to dexion keras};

bears the name.

(3) Lit. "and carved on the pedestal a representation of his own performances."

As our first topic we shall deal with the question, how a man may best avoid being cheated in the purchase of a horse.

Take the case of a foal as yet unbroken: it is plain that our scrutiny must begin with the body; an animal that has never yet been mounted can but present the vaguest indications of spirit. Confining ourselves therefore to the body, the first point to examine, we maintain, will be the feet. Just as a house would be of little use, however beautiful its upper stories, if the underlying foundations were not what they ought to be, so there is little use to be extracted from a horse, and in particular a war-horse, (4) if unsound in his feet, however excellent his other points; since he could not turn a single one of them to good account. (5)

(4) Or, "and that a charger, we will suppose." For the simile see "Mem." III. i. 7.

(5) Cf. Hor. "Sat." I. ii. 86:

regibus hic mos est: ubi equos mercantur, opertos inspiciunt, ne, si facies, ut saepe, decora molli fulta pede est, emptorem inducat hiantem, quod pulchrae clunes, breve quod caput, ardua cervix.

and see Virg. "Georg." iii. 72 foll.

In testing the feet the first thing to examine will be the horny portion of the hoof. For soundness of foot a thick horn is far better than a thin. Again it is important to notice whether the hoofs are high both before and behind, or flat to the ground; for a high hoof keeps the "frog," (6) as it is called, well off the ground; whereas a low hoof treads equally with the stoutest and softest part of the foot alike, the gait resembling that of a bandy-legged man. (7) "You may tell a good foot clearly by the ring," says Simon happily; (8) for the hollow hoof rings like a cymbal against the solid earth. (9)

(6) Lit. "the swallow."

(7) Al. "a knock-kneed person." See Stonehenge, "The Horse" (ed. 1892), pp. 3, 9.

(8) Or, "and he is right."

(9) Cf. Virg. "Georg." iii. 88; Hor. "Epod." xvi. 12.

And now that we have begun with the feet, let us ascend from this point to the rest of the body. The bones (10) above the hoof and below the fetlock must not be too straight, like those of a goat; through not being properly elastic, (11) legs of this type will jar the rider, and are more liable to become inflamed. On the other hand, these bones must not be too low, or else the fetlock will be abraded or lacerated when the horse is galloped over clods and stones.

(10) i.e. "the pasterns ({mesokunia}) and the coffin should be 'sloping.'"

(11) Or, "being too inflexible." Lit. "giving blow for blow, overuch like anvil to hammer."

The bones of the shanks (12) ought to be thick, being as they are the columns on which the body rests; thick in themselves, that is, not puffed out with veins or flesh; or else in riding over hard ground they will inevitably be surcharged with blood, and varicose conditions be set up, (13) the legs becoming thick and puffy, whilst the skin recedes; and with this loosening of the skin the back sinew (14) is very apt to start and render the horse lame.

(12) i.e. "the metacarpals and metatarsals."

(13)Or, "and become varicose, with the result that the shanks swell whilst the skin recedes from the bone."

(14)Or, "suspensory ligament"? Possibly Xenophon's anatomy is wrong, and he mistook the back sinew for a bone like the fibula. The part in question might intelligibly enough, if not technically, be termed {perone}, being of the brooch-pin order.

If the young horse in walking bends his knees flexibly, you may safely conjecture that when he comes to be ridden he will have flexible legs, since the quality of suppleness invariably increases with age. (15) Supple knees are highly esteemed and with good reason, rendering as they do the horse less liable to stumble or break down from fatigue than those of stiffer build.

(15) Lit. "all horses bend their legs more flexibly as time advances."

Coming to the thighs below the shoulder-blades, (16) or arms, these if thick and muscular present a stronger and handsomer appearance, just as in the case of a human being. Again, a comparatively broad chest is better alike for strength and beauty, and better adapted to carry the legs well asunder, so that they will not overlap and interfere with one another. Again, the neck should not be set on dropping forward from the chest, like a boar's, but, like that of a game-cock rather, it should shoot upwards to the crest, and be slack (17) along the curvature; whilst the head should be bony and the jawbone small. In this way the neck will be well in front of the rider, and the eye will command what lies before the horse's feet. A horse, moreover, of this build, however spirited, will be least capable of overmastering the rider, (18) since it is not by arching but by stretching out his neck and head that a horse endeavours to assert his power. (19)

(16)Lit. "the thighs below the shoulder-blades" are distinguished from "the thighs below the tail." They correspond respectively to our "arms" (i.e. forearms) and "gaskins," and anatomically speaking = the radius (os brachii) and the tibia.

(17) "Slack towards the flexure" (Stonehenge).

(18) Or, "of forcing the rider's hand and bolting."

(19) Or, "to display violence or run away."

It is important also to observe whether the jaws are soft or hard on one or other side, since as a rule a horse with unequal jaws (20) is liable to become hard-mouthed on one side.

(20) Or, "whose bars are not equally sensitive."

Again, a prominent rather than a sunken eye is suggestive of alertness, and a horse of this type will have a wider range of vision.

And so of the nostrils: a wide-dilated nostril is at once better than a contracted one for respiration, and gives the animal a fiercer aspect. Note how, for instance, when one stallion is enraged against another, or when his spirit chafes in being ridden, (21) the nostrils at once become dilated.

(21) Or, "in the racecourse or on the exercising-ground how readily he distends his nostrils."

A comparatively large crest and small ears give a more typical and horse-like appearance to the head, whilst lofty withers again allow the rider a surer seat and a stronger adhesion between the shoulders and the body. (22)

(22) Or if with L. D. ({kai to somati}), transl. "adhesion to the horse's shoulders."

A "double spine," (23) again, is at once softer to sit on than a single, and more pleasing to the eye. So, too, a fairly deep side somewhat rounded towards the belly (24) will render the animal at once easier to sit and stronger, and as a general rule better able to digest his food. (25)

(23) Reading after Courier {rakhis ge men}. See Virg. "Georg." iii. 87, "at duplex agitur per lumbos spina." "In a horse that is in good case, the back is broad, and the spine does not stick up like a ridge, but forms a kind of furrow on the back" (John Martyn); "a full back," as we say.

(24) Or, "in proportion to." See Courier ("Du Commandement de la Cavalerie at de l'Equitation": deux livres de Xenophon, traduits par un officier d'artillerie a cheval), note ad loc. p. 83.

(25) i.e. "and keep in good condition."

The broader and shorter the loins the more easily will the horse raise his forequarters and bring up his hindquarters under him. Given these points, moreover, the belly will appear as small as possible, a portion of the body which if large is partly a disfigurement and partly tends to make the horse less strong and capable of carrying weight. (26)

(26) Al. "more feeble at once and ponderous in his gait."

The quarters should be broad and fleshy in correspondence with the sides and chest, and if they are also firm and solid throughout they will be all the lighter for the racecourse, and will render the horse in every way more fleet.

To come to the thighs (and buttocks): (27) if the horse have these separated by a broad line of demarcation (28) he will be able to plant his hind-legs under him with a good gap between; (29) and in so doing will assume a posture (30) and a gait in action at once prouder and more firmly balanced, and in every way appear to the best advantage.

(27) Lit. "the thighs beneath the tail."

(28) Reading {plateia to gramme diorismenous ekhe}, sc. the perineum.
    Al. Courier (after Apsyrtus), op. cit. p. 14, {plateis te kai me
    diestrammenous}, "broad and not turned outwards."

(29) Or, "he will be sure to spread well behind," etc.

(30) {ton upobasin}, tech. of the crouching posture assumed by the
    horse for mounting or "in doing the demi-passade" (so Morgan, op.
    cit. p. 126).

The human subject would seem to point to this conclusion. When a man wants to lift anything from off the ground he essays to do so by bringing the legs apart and not by bringing them together.

A horse ought not to have large testicles, though that is not a point to be determined in the colt.

And now, as regards the lower parts, the hocks, (31) or shanks and fetlocks and hoofs, we have only to repeat what has been said already about those of the fore-legs.

(31) {ton katothen astragelon, e knemon}, lit. "the under (or hinder?)
    knuckle-bones (hocks?) or shins"; i.e. anatomically speaking, the
    os calcis, astragalus, tarsals, and metatarsal large and small.

I will here note some indications by which one may forecast the probable size of the grown animal. The colt with the longest shanks at the moment of being foaled will grow into the biggest horse; the fact being—and it holds of all the domestic quadrupeds (32)—that with advance of time the legs hardly increase at all, while the rest of the body grows uniformly up to these, until it has attained its proper symmetry.

(32) Cf. Aristot. "de Part. Anim." iv. 10; "H. A." ii. 1; Plin. "N.
    H." xi. 108.

Such is the type (33) of colt and such the tests to be applied, with every prospect of getting a sound-footed, strong, and fleshy animal fine of form and large of stature. If changes in some instances develop during growth, that need not prevent us from applying our tests in confidence. It far more often happens that an ugly-looking colt will turn out serviceable, (34) than that a foal of the above description will turn out ugly or defective.

(33) Lit. "by testing the shape of the colt in this way it seems to us
    the purchaser will get," etc.

(34) For the vulg. {eukhroastoi}, a doubtful word = "well coloured,"
    i.e. "sleek and healthy," L. & S. would read {eukhrooi} (cf. "Pol.
    Lac." v. 8). L. Dind. conj. {enrostoi}, "robust"; Schneid.
    {eukhrestoi}, "serviceable."

II

The right method of breaking a colt needs no description at our hands. (1) As a matter of state organisation, (2) cavalry duties usually devolve upon those who are not stinted in means, and who have a considerable share in the government; (3) and it seems far better for a young man to give heed to his own health of body and to horsemanship, or, if he already knows how to ride with skill, to practising manouvres, than that he should set up as a trainer of horses. (4) The older man has his town property and his friends, and the hundred-and-one concerns of state or of war, on which to employ his time and energies rather than on horsebreaking. It is plain then that any one holding my views (5) on the subject will put a young horse out to be broken. But in so doing he ought to draw up articles, just as a father does when he apprentices his son to some art or handicraft, stating what sort of knowledge the young creature is to be sent back possessed of. These will serve as indications (6) to the trainer what points he must pay special heed to if he is to earn his fee. At the same time pains should be taken on the owner's part to see that the colt is gentle, tractable, and affectionate, (7) when delivered to the professional trainer. That is a condition of things which for the most part may be brought about at home and by the groom—if he knows how to let the animal connect (8) hunger and thirst and the annoyance of flies with solitude, whilst associating food and drink and escape from sources of irritation with the presence of man. As the result of this treatment, necessarily the young horse will acquire—not fondness merely, but an absolute craving for human beings. A good deal can be done by touching, stroking, patting those parts of the body which the creature likes to have so handled. These are the hairiest parts, or where, if there is anything annoying him, the horse can least of all apply relief himself.

(1) Or, "The training of the colt is a topic which, as it seems to us, may fairly be omitted, since those appointed for cavalry service in these states are persons who," etc. For reading see Courier, "Notes," p. 84.

(2) "Organisation in the several states."

(3) Or, "As a matter of fact it is the wealthiest members of the state, and those who have the largest stake in civic life, that are appointed to cavalry duties." See "Hippparch," i. 9.

(4) Cf. "Econ." iii. 10.

(5) {ego}. Hitherto the author has used the plural {emin} with which he started.

(6) Reading {upodeigmata}, "finger-post signs," as it were, or "draft in outline"; al. {upomnemata} = "memoranda."

(7) "Gentle, and accustomed to the hand, and fond of man."

(8) Lit. "if he knows how to provide that hunger and thirst, etc., should be felt by the colt in solitude, whilst food and drink, etc., come through help of man."

The groom should have standing orders to take his charge through crowds, and to make him familiar with all sorts of sights and noises; and if the colt shows sign of apprehension at them, (9) he must teach him—not by cruel, but by gentle handling—that they are not really formidable.

Or, "is disposed to shy."

On this topic, then, of training, (10) the rules here given will, I think, suffice for any private individual.

(10) Or, "In reference to horsebreaking, the above remarks will
perhaps be found sufficient for the practical guidance of an
amateur."

III

To meet the case in which the object is to buy a horse already fit for riding, we will set down certain memoranda, (1) which, if applied intelligently, may save the purchaser from being cheated.

(1) "Which the purchaser should lay to heart, if he does not wish to
be cheated."

First, then, let there be no mistake about the age. If the horse has lost his mark teeth, (2) not only will the purchaser's hopes be blighted, but he may find himself saddled for ever with a sorry bargain. (3)

(2) Or, "the milk teeth," i.e. is more than five years old. See
Morgan, p. 126.

(3) Lit. "a horse that has lost his milk teeth cannot be said to
gladden his owner's mind with hopes, and is not so easily disposed
of."

Given that the fact of youth is well established, let there be no mistake about another matter: how does he take the bit into his mouth and the headstall (4) over his ears? There need be little ambiguity on this score, if the purchaser will see the bit inserted and again removed, under his eyes. Next, let it be carefully noted how the horse stands being mounted. Many horses are extremely loath to admit the approach of anything which, if once accepted, clearly means to them enforced exertion.

(4) {koruphaia}, part of the {khalinos} gear.

Another point to ascertain is whether the horse, when mounted, can be induced to leave other horses, or when being ridden past a group of horses standing, will not bolt off to join the company. Some horses again, as the result of bad training, will run away from the exercising-ground and make for the stable. A hard mouth may be detected by the exercise called the {pede} or volte, (5) and still more so by varying the direction of the volte to right or left. Many horses will not attempt to run away except for the concurrence of a bad mouth along with an avenue of escape home. (6)

(5) See Sturz, s.v.; Pollux, i. 219. Al. "the longe," but the passage
below (vii. 14) is suggestive rather of the volte.

(6) Al. "will only attempt to bolt where the passage out towards home
combines, as it were, with a bad mouth." {e… ekphora} = "the
exit from the manege or riding school."

Another point which it is necessary to learn is, whether when let go at full speed the horse can be pulled up (7) sharp and is willing to wheel round in obedience to the rein.

(7) {analambanetai}, "come to the poise" (Morgan). For
    {apostrephesthai} see ix.6; tech. "caracole."

It is also well to ascertain by experience if the horse you propose to purchase will show equal docility in response to the whip. Every one knows what a useless thing a servant is, or a body of troops, that will not obey. A disobedient horse is not only useless, but may easily play the part of an arrant traitor.

And since it is assumed that the horse to be purchased is intended for war, we must widen our test to include everything which war itself can bring to the proof: such as leaping ditches, scrambling over walls, scaling up and springing off high banks. We must test his paces by galloping him up and down steep pitches and sharp inclines and along a slant. For each and all of these will serve as a touchstone to gauge the endurance of his spirit and the soundness of his body.

I am far from saying, indeed, that because an animal fails to perform all these parts to perfection, he must straightway be rejected; since many a horse will fall short at first, not from inability, but from want of experience. With teaching, practice, and habit, almost any horse will come to perform all these feats beautifully, provided he be sound and free from vice. Only you must beware of a horse that is naturally of a nervous temperament. An over-timorous animal will not only prevent the rider from using the vantage-ground of its back to strike an enemy, but is as likely as not to bring him to earth himself and plunge him into the worst of straits.

We must, also, find out of the horse shows any viciousness towards other horses or towards human beings; also, whether he is skittish; (8) such defects are apt to cause his owner trouble.

(8) Or, "very ticklish."

As to any reluctance on the horse's part to being bitted or mounted, dancing and twisting about and the rest, (9) you will get a more exact idea on this score, if, when he has gone through his work, you will try and repeat the precise operations which he went through before you began your ride. Any horse that having done his work shows a readiness to undergo it all again, affords sufficient evidence thereby of spirit and endurance.

(9) Reading {talla dineumata}, lit. "and the rest of his twistings and
    twirlings about."

To put the matter in a nutshell: given that the horse is sound-footed, gentle, moderately fast, willing and able to undergo toil, and above all things (10) obedient—such an animal, we venture to predict, will give the least trouble and the greatest security to his rider in the circumstances of war; while, conversely, a beast who either out of sluggishness needs much driving, or from excess of mettle much coaxing and maneuvering, will give his rider work enough to occupy both his hands and a sinking of the heart when dangers thicken.

(10) Al. "thoroughly."

IV

We will now suppose the purchaser has found a horse which he admires; (1) the purchase is effected, and he has brought him home—how is he to be housed? It is best that the stable should be placed in a quarter of the establishment where the master will see the horse as often as possible. (2) It is a good thing also to have his stall so arranged that there will be as little risk of the horse's food being stolen from the manger, as of the master's from his larder or store-closet. To neglect a detail of this kind is surely to neglect oneself; since in the hour of danger, it is certain, the owner has to consign himself, life and limb, to the safe keeping of his horse.

(1) Lit. "To proceed: when you have bought a horse which you admire and have brought him home."

(2) i.e. "where he will be brought as frequently as possible under the master's eye." Cf. "Econ." xii. 20.

Nor is it only to avoid the risk of food being stolen that a secure horse-box is desirable, but for the further reason that if the horse takes to scattering his food, the action is at once detected; and any one who observes that happening may take it as a sign and symptom either of too much blood, (3) which calls for veterinary aid, or of over-fatigue, for which rest is the cure, or else that an attack of indigestion (4) or some other malady is coming on. And just as with human beings, so with the horse, all diseases are more curable at their commencement (5) than after they have become chronic, or been wrongly treated. (6)

(3) "A plethoric condition of the blood."

(4) {krithiasis}. Lit. "barley surfeit"; "une fourbure." See Aristot. "H. A." viii. 24. 4.

(5) i.e. "in the early acute stages."

(6) Al. "and the mischief has spread."

But if food and exercise with a view to strengthening the horse's body are matters of prime consideration, no less important is it to pay attention to the feet. A stable with a damp and smooth floor will spoil the best hoof which nature can give. (7) To prevent the floor being damp, it should be sloped with channels; and to avoid smoothness, paved with cobble stones sunk side by side in the ground and similar in size to the horse's hoofs. (8) A stable floor of this sort is calculated to strengthen the horse's feet by the mere pressure on the part in standing. In the next place it will be the groom's business to lead out the horse somewhere to comb and curry him; and after his morning's feed to unhalter him from the manger, (9) so that he may come to his evening meal with greater relish. To secure the best type of stable-yard, and with a view to strengthening the horse's feet, I would suggest to take and throw down loosely (10) four or five waggon loads of pebbles, each as large as can be grasped in the hand, and about a pound in weight; the whole to be fenced round with a skirting of iron to prevent scattering. The mere standing on these will come to precisely the same thing as if for a certain portion of the day the horse were, off and on, stepping along a stony road; whilst being curried or when fidgeted by flies he will be forced to use his hoofs just as much as if he were walking. Nor is it the hoofs merely, but a surface so strewn with stones will tend to harden the frog of the foot also.

(7) Lit. "A damp and smooth floor may be the ruin of a naturally good hoof." It will be understood that the Greeks did not shoe their horses.

(8) See Courier, p. 54, for an interesting experiment tried by himself at Bari.

(9) Cf. "Hipparch," i. 16.

(10) Or, "spread so as to form a surface."

But if care is needed to make the hoofs hard, similar pains should be taken to make the mouth and jaws soft; and the same means and appliances which will render a man's flesh and skin soft, will serve to soften and supple a horse's mouth. (11)

(11) Or, "may be used with like effect on a horse's mouth," i.e. bathing, friction, oil. See Pollux, i. 201.

V

It is the duty of a horseman, as we think, to have his groom trained thoroughly in all that concerns the treatment of the horse. In the first place, then, the groom should know that he is never to knot the halter (1) at the point where the headstall is attached to the horse's head. By constantly rubbing his head against the manger, if the halter does not sit quite loose about his ears, the horse will be constantly injuring himself; (2) and with sores so set up, it is inevitable that he should show peevishness, while being bitted or rubbed down.

(1) Lit. "by which the horse is tied to the manger"; "licol d'ecurie."

(2) Al. "in nine cases out of ten he rubs his head… and ten to one will make a sore."

It is desirable that the groom should be ordered to carry out the dung and litter of the horse to some one place each day. By so doing, he will discharge the duty with least trouble to himself, (3) and at the same time be doing the horse a kindness.

(3) Al. "get rid of the refuse in the easiest way."

The groom should also be instructed to attach the muzzle to the horse's mouth, both when taking him out to be groomed and to the rolling-ground. (4) In fact he should always muzzle him whenever he takes him anywhere without the bit. The muzzle, while it is no hindrance to respiration, prevents biting; and when attached it serves to rob the horse of opportunity for vice. (5)

(4) Cf. "Econ." xi. 18; Aristoph. "Clouds," 32.

(5) Or, "prevents the horse from carrying out vicious designs."

Again, care should be taken to tie the horse up with the halter above his head. A horse's natural instinct, in trying to rid himself of anything that irritates the face, is to toss up his head, and by this upward movement, if so tied, he only slackens the chain instead of snapping it. In rubbing the horse down, the groom should begin with the head and mane; as until the upper parts are clean, it is vain to cleanse the lower; then, as regards the rest of the body, first brush up the hair, by help of all the ordinary implements for cleansing, and then beat out the dust, following the lie of the hair. The hair on the spine (and dorsal region) ought not to be touched with any instrument whatever; the hand alone should be used to rub and smooth it, and in the direction of its natural growth, so as to preserve from injury that part of the horse's back on which the rider sits.

The head should be drenched with water simply; for, being bony, if you try to cleanse it with iron or wooden instruments injury may be caused. So, too, the forelock should be merely wetted; the long hairs of which it is composed, without hindering the animal's vision, serve to scare away from the eyes anything that might trouble them. Providence, we must suppose, (6) bestowed these hairs upon the horse, instead of the large ears which are given to the ass and the mule as a protection to the eyes. (7) The tail, again, and mane should be washed, the object being to help the hairs to grow—those in the tail so as to allow the creature the greatest reach possible in brushing away molesting objects, (8) and those of the neck in order that the rider may have as free a grip as possible.

(6) Lit. "The gods, we must suppose, gave…"

(7) Lit. "as defences or protective bulwarks."

(8) Insects, etc.

Mane, forelock, and tail are triple gifts bestowed by the gods upon the horse for the sake of pride and ornament, (9) and here is the proof: a brood mare, so long as her mane is long and flowing, will not readily suffer herself to be covered by an ass; hence breeders of mules take care to clip the mane of the mare with a view to covering. (10)

(9) {aglaias eneka} (a poetic word). Cf. "Od." xv. 78; xvii. 310.

(10) For this belief Schneid. cf Aristot. "H. A." vi. 18; Plin. viii. 42; Aelian, "H. A." ii. 10, xi. 18, xii. 16, to which Dr. Morgan aptly adds Soph. "Fr." 587 (Tyro), a beautiful passage, {komes de penthos lagkhano polou diken, k.t.l.} (cf. Plut. "Mor." 754 A).

Washing of the legs we are inclined to dispense with—no good is done but rather harm to the hoofs by this daily washing. So, too, excessive cleanliness of the belly is to be discouraged; the operation itself is most annoying to the horse; and the cleaner these parts are made, the thicker the swarm of troublesome things which collect beneath the belly. Besides which, however elaborately you clean these parts, the horse is no sooner led out than presently he will be just as dirty as if he had not been cleaned. Omit these ablutions then, we say; and similarly for the legs, rubbing and currying by hand is quite sufficient.

VI

We will now explain how the operation of grooming may be performed with least danger to oneself and best advantage to the horse. If the groom attempts to clean the horse with his face turned the same way as the horse, he runs the risk of getting a knock in the face from the animal's knee or hoof. When cleaning him he should turn his face in the opposite direction to the horse, and planting himself well out of the way of his leg, at an angle to his shoulder-blade, proceed to rub him down. He will then escape all mischief, and he will be able to clean the frog by folding back the hoof. Let him clean the hind-legs in the same way.

The man who has to do with the horse should know, with regard to this and all other necessary operations, that he ought to approach as little as possible from the head or the tail to perform them; for if the horse attempt to show vice he is master of the man in front and rear. But by approaching from the side he will get the greatest hold over the horse with the least risk of injury to himself.

When the horse has to be led, we do not approve of leading him from in front, for the simple reason that the person so leading him robs himself of his power of self-protection, whilst he leaves the horse freedom to do what he likes. On the other hand, we take a like exception to the plan of training the horse to go forward on a long rein (1) and lead the way, and for this reason: it gives the horse the opportunity of mischief, in whichever direction he likes, on either flank, and the power also to turn right about and face his driver. How can a troop of horses be kept free of one another, if driven in this fashion from behind?—whereas a horse accustomed to be led from the side will have least power of mischief to horse or man, and at the same time be in the best position to be mounted by the rider at a moment's notice, were it necessary.

(1) See a passage from Strattis, "Chrys." 2 (Pollux, x. 55), {prosage ton polon atrema, proslabon ton agogea brakhuteron. oukh oras oti abolos estin}.

In order to insert the bit correctly the groom should, in the first place, approach on the near (2) side of the horse, and then throwing the reins over his head, let them drop loosely on the withers; raise the headstall in his right hand, and with his left present the bit. If the horse will take the bit, it is a simple business to adjust the strap of the headstall; but if he refuses to open his mouth, the groom must hold the bit against the teeth and at the same time insert the thumb (3) of his left hand inside the horse's jaws. Most horses will open their mouths to that operation. But if he still refuses, then the groom must press the lip against the tush (4); very few horses will refuse the bit, when that is done to them. (5)

(2) Lit. "on the left-hand side."

(3) {ton megan daktulon}, Hdt. iii. 8.

(4) i.e. "canine tooth."

(5) Or, "it is a very exceptional horse that will not open his mouth under the circumstances."

The groom can hardly be too much alive to the following points * * * if any work is to be done: (6) in fact, so important is it that the horse should readily take his bit, that, to put it tersely, a horse that will not take it is good for nothing. Now, if the horse be bitted not only when he has work to do, but also when he is being taken to his food and when he is being led home from a ride, it would be no great marvel if he learnt to take the bit of his own accord, when first presented to him.

(6) Reading with L. Dind. {khre de ton ippokomon kai ta oiade... paroxunthai, ei ti dei ponein}, or if as Schneid., Sauppe, etc., {khre de ton ippon me kata toiade, k.t.l.}, transl. "the horse must not be irritated in such operations as these," etc.; but {toiade} = "as follows," if correct, suggests a lacuna in either case at this point.

It would be good for the groom to know how to give a leg up in the Persian fashion, (7) so that in case of illness or infirmity of age the master himself may have a man to help him on to horseback without trouble, or, if he so wish, be able to oblige a friend with a man to mount him. (8)

(7) Cf. "Anab." IV. iv. 4; "Hipparch," i. 17; "Cyrop." VII. i. 38.

(8) An {anaboleus}. Cf. Plut. "C. Gracch." 7.

The one best precept—the golden rule—in dealing with a horse is never to approach him angrily. Anger is so devoid of forethought that it will often drive a man to do things which in a calmer mood he will regret. (9) Thus, when a horse is shy of any object and refuses to approach it, you must teach him that there is nothing to be alarmed at, particularly if he be a plucky animal; (10) or, failing that, touch the formidable object yourself, and then gently lead the horse up to it. The opposite plan of forcing the frightened creature by blows only intensifies its fear, the horse mentally associating the pain he suffers at such a moment with the object of suspicion, which he naturally regards as its cause.

(9) Cf. "Hell." v. iii. 7 for this maxim.

(10) Al. "if possibly by help of another and plucky animal."

If, when the groom brings up the horse to his master to mount, he knows how to make him lower his back, (11) to facilitate mounting, we have no fault to find. Still, we consider that the horseman should practise and be able to mount, even if the horse does not so lend himself; (12) since on another occasion another type of horse may fall to the rider's lot, (13) nor can the same rider be always served by the same equerry. (14)

(11) {upobibazesthai}. See above, i. 14; Pollux, i. 213; Morgan ad loc. "Stirrups were unknown till long after the Christian era began."

(12) Or, "apart from these good graces on the animal's part."

(13) As a member of the cavalry.

(14) Reading {allo}. Al. reading {allos} with L. D., "and the same horse will at one time humour you in one way and again in another." Cf. viii. 13, x. 12, for {uperetein} of the horse.

VII

The master, let us suppose, has received his horse and is ready to mount. (1) We will now prescribe certain rules to be observed in the interests not only of the horseman but of the animal which he bestrides. First, then, he should take the leading rein, which hangs from the chin-strap or nose-band, (2) conveniently in his left hand, held slack so as not to jerk the horse's mouth, whether he means to mount by hoisting himself up, catching hold of the mane behind the ears, or to vault on to horseback by help of his spear. With the right hand he should grip the reins along with a tuft of hair beside the shoulder-joint, (3) so that he may not in any way wrench the horse's mouth with the bit while mounting. In the act of taking the spring off the ground for mounting, (4) he should hoist his body by help of the left hand, and with the right at full stretch assist the upward movement (5) (a position in mounting which will present a graceful spectacle also from behind); (6) at the same time with the leg well bent, and taking care not to place his knee on the horse's back, he must pass his leg clean over to the off side; and so having brought his foot well round, plant himself firmly on his seat. (7)

(1) Reading {otan… paradexetai… os anabesomenos}. Or,
    reading {otan paradexetai ton ippea (sc. o. ippos) ws
    anabesomenon}, transl. "the horse has been brought round ready for
    mounting."

(2) So Courier, "la muserolle." It might be merely a stitched leather
    strap or made of a chain in part, which rattled; as
    {khrusokhalinon patagon psalion} (Aristoph. "Peace," 155) implies.
    "Curb" would be misleading.

(3) "Near the withers."

(4) Or, "as soon as he has got the springing poise preliminary to
    mounting."

(5) "Give himself simultaneously a lift." Reading {ekteinon}, or if
    {enteinon}, "keeping his right arm stiff."

(6) Or, "a style of mounting which will obviate an ungainly attitude
    behind."

(7) Lit. "lower his buttocks on to the horse's back."

To meet the case in which the horseman may chance to be leading his horse with the left hand and carrying his spear in the right, it would be good, we think, for every one to practise vaulting on to his seat from the right side also. In fact, he has nothing else to learn except to do with his right limbs what he has previously done with the left, and vice versa. And the reason we approve of this method of mounting is (8) that it enables the soldier at one and the same instant to get astride of his horse and to find himself prepared at all points, supposing he should have to enter the lists of battle on a sudden.

(8) Lit. "One reason for the praise which we bestow on this method of
    mounting is that at the very instant of gaining his seat the
    soldier finds himself fully prepared to engage the enemy on a
    sudden, if occasion need."

But now, supposing the rider fairly seated, whether bareback or on a saddle-cloth, a good seat is not that of a man seated on a chair, but rather the pose of a man standing upright with his legs apart. In this way he will be able to hold on to the horse more firmly by his thighs; and this erect attitude will enable him to hurl a javelin or to strike a blow from horseback, if occasion calls, with more vigorous effect. The leg and foot should hang loosely from the knee; by keeping the leg stiff, the rider is apt to have it broken in collision with some obstacle; whereas a flexible leg (9) will yield to the impact, and at the same time not shift the thigh from its position. The rider should also accustom the whole of his body above the hips to be as supple as possible; for thus he will enlarge his scope of action, and in case of a tug or shove be less liable to be unseated. Next, when the rider is seated, he must, in the first place, teach his horse to stand quiet, until he has drawn his skirts from under him, if need be, (10) and got the reins an equal length and grasped his spear in the handiest fashion; and, in the next place, he should keep his left arm close to his side. This position will give the rider absolute ease and freedom, (11) and his hand the firmest hold.

(9) i.e. "below the knee"; "shin and calf."

(10) Lit. "pulled up" (and arranged the folds of his mantle).

(11) {eustalestatos}, "the most business-like deportment."

As to reins, we recommend those which are well balanced, without being weak or slippery or thick, so that when necessary, the hand which holds them can also grasp a spear.

As soon as the rider gives the signal to the horse to start, (12) he should begin at a walking pace, which will tend to allay his excitement. If the horse is inclined to droop his head, the reins should be held pretty high; or somewhat low, if he is disposed to carry his head high. This will set off the horse's bearing to the best advantage. Presently, as he falls into a natural trot, (13) he will gradually relax his limbs without the slightest suffering, and so come more agreeably to the gallop. (14) Since, too, the preference is given to starting on the left foot, it will best conduce to that lead if, while the horse is still trotting, the signal to gallop should be given at the instant of making a step with his right foot. (15) As he is on the point of lifting his left foot he will start upon it, and while turning left will simultaneously make the first bound of the gallop; (16) since, as a matter of instinct, a horse, on being turned to the right, leads off with his right limbs, and to the left with his left.

(12) "Forwards!"

(13) Or, "the true trot."

(14) {epirrabdophorein}, "a fast pace in response to a wave of the whip."

(15) See Berenger, i. p. 249; also the "Cavalry Drill Book," Part I. Equitation, S. 22, "The Canter."

(16) {tes episkeliseos}, "he will make the forward stride of the gallop in the act of turning to the left." See Morgan ad loc.

As an exercise, we recommend what is called the volte, (17) since it habituates the animal to turn to either hand; while a variation in the order of the turn is good as involving an equalisation of both sides of the mouth, in first one, and then the other half of the exercise. (18) But of the two we commend the oval form of the volte rather than the circular; for the horse, being already sated with the straight course, will be all the more ready to turn, and will be practised at once in the straight course and in wheeling. At the curve, he should be held up, (19) because it is neither easy nor indeed safe when the horse is at full speed to turn sharp, especially if the ground is broken (20) or slippery.

(17) {pede}, figure of eight.

(18) Or, "on first one and then the other half of the manege."

(19) {upolambanein}. See "Hipparch," iii. 14; "Hunting," iii. 10; vi. 22, of a dog.

(20) {apokroton}, al. {epikroton}, "beaten, hard-trodden ground."

But in collecting him, the rider should as little as possible sway the horse obliquely with the bit, and as little as possible incline his own body; or, he may rest assured, a trifle will suffice to stretch him and his horse full length upon the ground. The moment the horse has his eyes fixed on the straight course after making a turn, is the time to urge him to full speed. In battle, obviously, these turns and wheelings are with a view to charging or retiring; consequently, to practise quickening the pace after wheeling is desirable. When the horse seems to have had enough of the manege, it would be good to give him a slight pause, and then suddenly to put him to his quickest, away from his fellows first, (21) and now towards them; and then again to quiet him down in mid-career as short as possible; (22) and from halt once more to turn him right-about and off again full charge. It is easy to predict that the day will come when there will be need of each of these manouvres.

(21) {mentoi}, "of course."

(22) Or, "within the narrowest compass"; "as finely as possible."

When the moment to dismount has come, you should never do so among other horses, nor near a group of people, (23) nor outside the exercising-ground; but on the precise spot which is the scene of his compulsory exertion there let the horse find also relaxation. (24)

(23) Or, "a knot of bystanders"; cf. Thuc. ii. 21.

(24) Or, as we say, "be caressed, and dismissed."

VIII

As there will, doubtless, be times when the horse will need to race downhill and uphill and on sloping ground; times, also, when he will need to leap across an obstacle; or, take a flying leap from off a bank; (1) or, jump down from a height, the rider must teach and train himself and his horse to meet all emergencies. In this way the two will have a chance of saving each the other, and may be expected to increase their usefulness.

(1) {ekpedan} = exsilire in altum (Sturz, and so Berenger); "to leap over ditches, and upon high places and down from them."

And here, if any reader should accuse us of repeating ourselves, on the ground that we are only stating now what we said before on the same topics,

(2) we say that this is not mere repetition. In the former case, we confined ourselves to advising the purchaser before he concluded his bargain to test whether the horse could do those particular things; (3) what we are now maintaining is that the owner ought to teach his own horse, and we will explain how this teaching is to be done.

(2) Or, "treating of a topic already handled."

(3) i.e. possessed a certain ability at the date of purchase.

With a horse entirely ignorant of leaping, the best way is to take him by the leading rein, which hangs loose, and to get across the trench yourself first, and then to pull tight on the leading-rein, to induce him to leap across. If he refuses, some one with a whip or switch should apply it smartly. The result will be that the horse will clear at a bound, not the distance merely, but a far larger space than requisite; and for the future there will be no need for an actual blow, the mere sight of some one coming up behind will suffice to make him leap. As soon as he is accustomed to leap in this way you may mount him and put him first at smaller and then at larger trenches. At the moment of the spring be ready to apply the spur; and so too, when training him to leap up and leap down, you should touch him with the spur at the critical instant. In the effort to perform any of these actions with the whole body, the horse will certainly perform them with more safety to himself and to his rider than he will, if his hind-quarters lag, in taking a ditch or fence, or in making an upward spring or downward jump. (4)

(4) Lit. "in making these jumps, springs, and leaps across or up or down."

To face a steep incline, you must first teach him on soft ground, and finally, when he is accustomed to that, he will much prefer the downward to the upward slope for a fast pace. And as to the apprehension, which some people entertain, that a horse may dislocate the shoulder in galloping down an incline, it should encourage them to learn that the Persians and Odrysians all run races down precipitous slopes; (5) and their horses are every bit as sound as our own. (6)

(5) Cf. "Anab." IV. viii. 28; and so the Georgians to this day (Chardin ap. Courier, op. cit. p. 70, n. 1).

(6) Lit. "as are those of the Hellenes."

Nor must we omit another topic: how the rider is to accommodate himself to these several movements. (7) Thus, when the horse breaks off into a gallop, the rider ought to bend forward, since the horse will be less likely to slip from under; and so to pitch his rider off. So again in pulling him up short (8) the rider should lean back; and thus escape a shock. In leaping a ditch or tearing up a steep incline, it is no bad plan to let go the reins and take hold of the mane, so that the animal may not feel the burthen of the bit in addition to that of the ground. In going down a steep incline the rider must throw himself right back and hold in the horse with the bit, to prevent himself being hurled headforemost down the slope himself if not his horse.

(7) Or, "to each set of occurrences."

(8) Al. "when the horse is being brought to a poise" (Morgan), and see Hermann ap. Schneid., {analambanein} = retinere equum, anhalten, pariren. i.e. "rein in" of the "Parade."

It is a correct principle to vary these exercises, which should be gone through sometimes in one place and sometimes in another, and should sometimes be shorter and sometimes longer in duration. The horse will take much more kindly to them if you do not confine him to one place and one routine.

Since it is a matter of prime necessity that the rider should keep his seat, while galloping full speed on every sort of ground, and at the same time be able to use his weapons with effect on horseback, nothing could be better, where the country suits and there are wild animals, than to practise horsemanship in combination with the chase. But when these resources fail, a good exercise may be supplied in the combined efforts of two horsemen. (9) One of them will play the part of fugitive, retreating helter-skelter over every sort of ground, with lance reversed and plying the butt end. The other pursues, with buttons on his javelins and his lance similarly handled. (10) Whenever he comes within javelin range he lets fly at the retreating foeman with his blunted missiles; or whenever within spear thrust he deals the overtaken combatant a blow. In coming to close quarters, it is a good plan first to drag the foeman towards oneself, and then on a sudden to thrust him off; that is a device to bring him to the ground. (11) The correct plan for the man so dragged is to press his horse forward: by which action the man who is being dragged is more likely to unhorse his assailant than to be brought to the ground himself.

(9) {ippota}. A poetic word; "cavaliers."

(10) Or, "manipulated."

(11) Or, "that may be spoken off as the 'purl trick'"; "it will unhorse him if anything."

If it ever happens that you have an enemy's camp in front, and cavalry skirmishing is the order of the day (at one time charging the enemy right up to the hostile battle-line, and again beating a retreat), under these circumstances it is well to bear in mind that so long as the skirmisher is close to his own party, (12) valour and discretion alike dictate to wheel and charge in the vanguard might and main; but when he finds himself in close proximity to the foe, he must keep his horse well in hand. This, in all probability, will enable him to do the greatest mischief to the enemy, and to receive least damage at his hands.

(12) See "Hipparch," viii. 23.

The gods have bestowed on man, indeed, the gift of teaching man his duty by means of speech and reasoning, but the horse, it is obvious, is not open to instruction by speech and reasoning. If you would have a horse learn to perform his duty, your best plan will be, whenever he does as you wish, to show him some kindness in return, and when he is disobedient to chastise him. This principle, though capable of being stated in a few words, is one which holds good throughout the whole of horsemanship. As, for instance, a horse will more readily take the bit, if each time he accepts it some good befalls him; or, again, he will leap ditches and spring up embankments and perform all the other feats incumbent on him, if he be led to associate obedience to the word of command with relaxation. (13)

(13) Lit. "if every time he performs the word of command he is led to expect some relaxation."

IX

The topics hitherto considered have been: firstly, how to reduce the chance of being cheated in the purchase of a colt or full-grown horse; secondly, how to escape as much as possible the risk of injuring your purchase by mishandling; and lastly, how to succeed in turning out a horse possessed of all the qualities demanded by the cavalry soldier for the purposes of war.

The time has come perhaps to add a few suggestions, in case the rider should be called upon to deal with an animal either unduly spirited or again unduly sluggish in disposition. The first point to recognise is, that temper of spirit in a horse takes the place of passion or anger in a man; and just as you may best escape exciting a man's ill-temper by avoiding harshness of speech and act, so you will best avoid enraging a spirited horse by not annoying him. Thus, from the first instant, in the act of mounting him, you should take pains to minimise the annoyance; and once on his back you should sit quiet for longer than the ordinary time, and so urge him forward by the gentlest signs possible; next, beginning at the slowest pace, gradually work him into a quicker step, but so gradually that he will find himself at full speed without noticing it. (1) Any sudden signal will bewilder a spirited horse, just as a man is bewildered by any sudden sight or sound or other experience. (I say one should be aware that any unexpected shock will produce disturbance in a horse.) (2)

(1) Or, "so that the horse may insensibly fall into a gallop."

(2) L. Dindorf and others bracket, as spurious.

So if you wish to pull up a spirited horse when breaking off into a quicker pace than requisite, you must not suddenly wrench him, but quietly and gently bring the bit to bear upon him, coaxing him rather than compelling him to calm down. It is the long steady course rather than the frequent turn which tends to calm a horse. (3) A quiet pace sustained for a long time has a caressing, (4) soothing effect, the reverse of exciting. If any one proposes by a series of fast and oft-repeated gallops to produce a sense of weariness in the horse, and so to tame him, his expectation will not be justified by the result; for under such circumstances a spirited horse will do his best to carry the day by main force, (5) and with a show of temper, like a passionate man, may contrive to bring on himself and his rider irreparable mischief.

(3) Or, "long stretches rather than a succession of turns and counter turns," {apostrophai}.

(4) Reading {katapsosi} with L. Dind.

(5) {agein bia}, vi agere, vi uti, Sturz; al. "go his own gait by sheer force."

A spirited horse should be kept in check, so that he does not dash off at full speed; and on the same principle, you should absolutely abstain from setting him to race against another; as a general rule, your fiery-spirited horse is only too fond of contention. (6)

(6) Reading {skhedon gar kai phil oi thum}, or if {... oi thil kai th.} transl. "the more eager and ambitious a horse is, the more mettlesome he will tend to become."

Smooth bits are better and more serviceable than rough; if a rough bit be inserted at all, it must be made to resemble a smooth one as much as possible by lightness of hand.

It is a good thing also for the rider to accustom himself to keep a quiet seat, especially when mounted on a spirited horse; and also to touch him as little as possible with anything except that part of the body necessary to secure a firm seat.

Again, it should be known that the conventional "chirrup" (7) to quiet and "cluck" to rouse a horse are a sort of precept of the training school; and supposing any one from the beginning chose to associate soft soothing actions with the "cluck" sound, and harsh rousing actions with the "chirrup," the horse could be taught to rouse himself at the "chirrup" and to calm himself at the "cluck" sound. On this principle, at the sound of the trumpet or the shout of battle the rider should avoid coming up to his charger in a state of excitement, or, indeed, bringing any disturbing influence to bear on the animal. As far as possible, at such a crisis he should halt and rest him; and, if circumstances permit, give him his morning or his evening meal. But the best advice of all is not to get an over-spirited horse for the purposes of war.

(7) Al. "whistling," and see Berenger, ii. 68. {poppusmos}, a sound from the lips; {klogmos}, from the cheek.

As to the sluggish type of animal, I need only suggest to do everything the opposite to what we advise as appropriate in dealing with an animal of high spirit.

X

But possibly you are not content with a horse serviceable for war. You want to find him him a showy, attractive animal, with a certain grandeur of bearing. If so, you must abstain from pulling at his mouth with the bit, or applying the spur and whip—methods commonly adopted by people with a view to a fine effect, though, as a matter of fact, they thereby achieve the very opposite of what they are aiming at. That is to say, by dragging the mouth up they render the horse blind instead of alive to what is in front of him; and what with spurring and whipping they distract the creature to the point of absolute bewilderment and danger. (1) Feats indeed!—the feats of horses with a strong dislike to being ridden—up to all sorts of ugly and ungainly tricks. On the contrary, let the horse be taught to be ridden on a loose bridle, and to hold his head high and arch his neck, and you will practically be making him perform the very acts which he himself delights or rather exults in; and the best proof of the pleasure which he takes is, that when he is let loose with other horses, and more particularly with mares, you will see him rear his head aloft to the full height, and arch his neck with nervous vigour, (2) pawing the air with pliant legs (3) and waving his tail on high. By training him to adopt the very airs and graces which he naturally assumes when showing off to best advantage, you have got what you are aiming at—a horse that delights in being ridden, a splendid and showy animal, the joy of all beholders.

(1) Al. "the animals are so scared that, the chances are, they are thrown into disorder."

(2) {gorgoumenos}, with pride and spirit, but with a suggestion of "fierceness and rage," as of Job's war-horse.

(3) "Mollia crura reponit," Virg. "Georg." iii. 76; Hom. "Hymn. ad Merc."

How these desirable results are, in our opinion, to be produced, we will now endeavour to explain. In the first place, then, you ought to have at least two bits. One of these should be smooth, with discs of a good size; the other should have heavy and flat discs (4) studded with sharp spikes, so that when the horse seizes it and dislikes the roughness he will drop it; then when the smooth is given him instead, he is delighted with its smoothness, and whatever he has learnt before upon the rough, he will perform with greater relish on the smooth. He may certainly, out of contempt for its very smoothness, perpetually try to get a purchase on it, and that is why we attach large discs to the smooth bit, the effect of which is to make him open his mouth, and drop the mouthpiece. It is possible to make the rough bit of every degree of roughness by keeping it slack or taut.

(4) See Morgan, op. cit. p. 144 foll.

But, whatever the type of bit may be, let it in any case be flexible. If it be stiff, at whatever point the horse seizes it he must take it up bodily against his jaws; just as it does not matter at what point a man takes hold of a bar of iron, (5) he lifts it as a whole. The other flexibly constructed type acts like a chain (only the single point at which you hold it remains stiff, the rest hangs loose); and while perpetually hunting for the portion which escapes him, he lets the mouthpiece go from his bars. (6) For this reason the rings are hung in the middle from the two axles, (7) so that while feeling for them with his tongue and teeth he may neglect to take the bit up against his jaws.

(5) Or, "poker," as we might say; lit. "spit."

(6) Schneid. cf. Eur. "Hippol." 1223.

(7) See Morgan, note ad loc. Berenger (i. 261) notes: "We have a small chain in the upset or hollow part of our bits, called a 'Player,' with which the horse playing with his tongue, and rolling it about, keeps his mouth moist and fresh; and, as Xenophon hints, it may serve likewise to fix his attention and prevent him from writhing his mouth about, or as the French call it, 'faire ses forces.'"

To explain what is meant by flexible and stiff as applied to a bit, we will describe the matter. A flexible bit is one in which the axles have their points of junction broad and smooth, (8) so as to bend easily; and where the several parts fitting round the axles, being large of aperture and not too closely packed, have greater flexibility; whereas, if the several parts do not slide to and fro with ease, and play into each other, that is what we call a stiff bit. Whatever the kind of bit may be, the rider must carry out precisely the same rules in using it, as follows, if he wishes to turn out a horse with the qualities described. The horse's mouth is not to be pulled back too harshly so as to make him toss his head aside, nor yet so gently that he will not feel the pressure. But the instant he raises his neck in answer to the pull, give him the bit at once; and so throughout, as we never cease repeating, at every response to your wishes, whenever and wherever the animal performs his service well,
(9) reward and humour him. Thus, when the rider perceives that the horse takes a pleasure in the high arching and supple play of his neck, let him seize the instant not to impose severe exertion on him, like a taskmaster, but rather to caress and coax him, as if anxious to give him a rest. In this way the horse will be encouraged and fall into a rapid pace.

(8) i.e. "the ends of the axles (at the point of junction) which work into each other are broad and smooth, so as to play freely at the join."

(9) "Behaves compliantly."

That a horse takes pleasure in swift movement, may be shown conclusively.

As soon as he has got his liberty, he sets off at a trot or gallop, never at a walking pace; so natural and instinctive a pleasure does this action afford him, if he is not forced to perform it to excess; since it is true of horse and man alike that nothing is pleasant if carried to excess. (10)

(10) L. Dind. cf. Eur. "Med." 128, {ta de' uperballont oudena kairon}.

But now suppose he has attained to the grand style when ridden—we have accustomed him of course in his first exercise to wheel and fall into a canter simultaneously; assuming then, he has got that lesson well by heart, if the rider pulls him up with the bit while simultaneously giving him one of the signals to be off, the horse, galled on the one hand by the bit, and on the other collecting himself in obedience to the signal "off," will throw forward his chest and raise his legs aloft with fiery spirit; though not indeed with suppleness, for the supple play of the limbs ceases as soon as the horse feels annoyance. But now, supposing when his fire is thus enkindled (11) you give him the rein, the effect is instantaneous. Under the pleasurable sense of freedom, thanks to the relaxation of the bit, with stately bearing and legs pliantly moving he dashes forward in his pride, in every respect imitating the airs and graces of a horse approaching other horses. Listen to the epithets with which spectators will describe the type of horse: the noble animal! and what willingness to work, what paces, (12) what a spirit and what mettle; how proudly he bears himself (13)—a joy at once, and yet a terror to behold.

(11) Cf. "Hell." V. iv. 46, "kindled into new life."

(12) {ipposten}, "a true soldier's horse."

(13) {sobaron}, "what a push and swagger"; {kai ama edun te kai gorgon idein}, "a la fois doux et terrible a voir," see Victor Cherbuliez, "Un Cheval de Phidias," p. 148.

Thus far on this topic; these notes may serve perhaps to meet a special need.

XI

If, however, the wish is to secure a horse adapted to parade and state processions, a high stepper and a showy (1) animal, these are qualities not to be found combined in every horse, but to begin with, the animal must have high spirit and a stalwart body. Not that, as some think, a horse with flexible legs will necessarily be able to rear his body. What we want is a horse with supple loins, and not supple only but short and strong (I do not mean the loins towards the tail, but by the belly the region between the ribs and thighs). That is the horse who will be able to plant his hind-legs well under the forearm. If while he is so planting his hind-quarters, he is pulled up with the bit, he lowers his hind-legs on his hocks (2) and raises the forepart of his body, so that any one in front of him will see the whole length of his belly to the sheath. (3) At the moment the horse does this, the rider should give him the rein, so that he may display the noblest feats which a horse can perform of his own free will, to the satisfaction of the spectators.

(1) {lampros}. Cf. Isae. xi. 41 ("On the estate of Hagnias"), Lys. xix. 63 ("de Bon. Arist.").

(2) See Berenger, ii. 68.

(3) Lit. "testicles."

There are, indeed, other methods of teaching these arts. (4) Some do so by touching the horse with a switch under the hocks, others employ an attendant to run alongside and strike the horse with a stick under the gaskins. For ourselves, however, far the best method of instruction, (5) as we keep repeating, is to let the horse feel that whatever he does in obedience to the rider's wishes will be followed by some rest and relaxation.

(4) Lit. "People, it must be admitted, claim to teach these arts in various ways—some by… others by bidding…"

(5) Reading {didaskalion}, al. {didaskalion}, "systems." Schneid. cf. Herod. v. 58.

To quote a dictum of Simon, what a horse does under compulsion he does blindly, and his performance is no more beautiful than would be that of a ballet-dancer taught by whip and goad. The performances of horse or man so treated would seem to be displays of clumsy gestures rather than of grace and beauty. What we need is that the horse should of his own accord exhibit his finest airs and paces at set signals. (6) Supposing, when he is in the riding-field, (7) you push him to a gallop until he is bathed in sweat, and when he begins to prance and show his airs to fine effect, you promptly dismount and take off the bit, you may rely upon it he will of his own accord another time break into the same prancing action. Such are the horses on which gods and heroes ride, as represented by the artist. The majesty of men themselves is best discovered in the graceful handling of such animals. (8) A horse so prancing is indeed a thing of beauty, a wonder and a marvel; riveting the gaze of all who see him, young alike and graybeards. They will never turn their backs, I venture to predict, or weary of their gazing so long as he continues to display his splendid action.

(6) Or, "by aids and signs," as we say.

(7) Or, "exercising-ground."

(8) Or, "and the man who knows how to manage such a creature gracefully himself at once appears magnificent."

If the possessor of so rare a creature should find himself by chance in the position of a squadron leader or a general of cavalry, he must not confine his zeal to the development of his personal splendour, but should study all the more to make the troop or regiment a splendid spectacle. Supposing (in accordance with the high praise bestowed upon the type of animal) (9) the leader is mounted on a horse which with his high airs and frequent prancing makes but the slightest movement forward—obviously the rest of the troop must follow at a walking pace, and one may fairly ask where is the element of splendour in the spectacle? But now suppose that you, sir, being at the head of the procession, rouse your horse and take the lead at a pace neither too fast nor yet too slow, but in a way to bring out the best qualities in all the animals, their spirit, fire, grace of mien and bearing ripe for action—I say, if you take the lead of them in this style, the collective thud, the general neighing and the snorting of the horses will combine to render not only you at the head, but your whole company (10) down to the last man a thrilling spectacle.

(9) Reading as vulg. {os malista epainousi tous toioutous ippous, os}.
   L. Dind. omits the words as a gloss.

(10)Reading {oi} (for {osoi}) {sumparepomenoi}. See Hartmann, "An.
   Xen. Nov." xiv. p. 343.

One word more. Supposing a man has shown some skill in purchasing his horses, and can rear them into strong and serviceable animals, supposing further he can handle them in the right way, not only in the training for war, but in exercises with a view to display, or lastly, in the stress of actual battle, what is there to prevent such a man from making every horse he owns of far more value in the end than when he bought it, with the further outlook that, unless some power higher than human interpose, (11) he will become the owner of a celebrated stable, and himself as celebrated for his skill in horsemanship.

(11)Or, "there is nothing, humanly speaking, to prevent such a man."
   For the phrase see "Mem." I. iii. 5; cf. "Cyrop." I. vi. 18; and
   for the advice, "Econ." iii. 9, 10.

XII

We will now describe the manner in which a trooper destined to run the risks of battle upon horseback should be armed. In the first place, then, we would insist, the corselet must be made to fit the person; since, if it fits well, its weight will be distributed over the whole body; whereas, if too loose, the shoulders will have all the weight to bear, while, if too tight, the corselet is no longer a defensive arm, but a "strait jacket." (1) Again, the neck, as being a vital part, (2) ought to have, as we maintain, a covering, appended to the corselet and close-fitting. This will serve as an ornament, and if made as it ought to be, will conceal the rider's face—if so he chooses—up to the nose.

(1) Cf. "Mem." III. x.

(2) L. Dind. cf. Hom. "Il." viii. 326:

{... othi kleis apoergei aukhena te stethos te, malista de kairion estin.}

"Where the collar-bone fenceth off neck and breast, and where is the most deadly spot" (W. Leaf).

As to the helmet, the best kind, in our opinion, is one of the Boeotian pattern, (3) on the principle again, that it covers all the parts exposed above the breastplate without hindering vision. Another point: the corselet should be so constructed that it does not prevent its wearer sitting down or stooping. About the abdomen and the genitals and parts surrounding (4) flaps should be attached in texture and in thickness sufficient to protect (5) that region.

(3) Schneider cf. Aelian, "V. H." iii. 24; Pollux, i. 149.

(4) Schneider cf. "Anab." IV. vii. 15, and for {kai ta kuklo}, conj. {kuklo}, "the abdomen and middle should be encircled by a skirt."

(5) Lit. "let there be wings of such sort, size, and number as to protect the limbs."

Again, as an injury to the left hand may disable the horseman, we would recommend the newly-invented piece of armour called the gauntlet, which protects the shoulder, arm, and elbow, with the hand engaged in holding the reins, being so constructed as to extend and contract; in addition to which it covers the gap left by the corselet under the armpit. The case is different with the right hand, which the horseman must needs raise to discharge a javelin or strike a blow. Here, accordingly, any part of the corselet which would hinder action out to be removed; in place of which the corselet ought to have some extra flaps (6) at the joints, which as the outstretched arm is raised unfold, and as the arm descends close tight again. The arm itself, (7) it seems to us, will better be protected by a piece like a greave stretched over it than bound up with the corselet. Again, the part exposed when the right hand is raised should be covered close to the corselet either with calfskin or with metal; or else there will be a want of protection just at the most vital point.

(6) {prosthetai}, "moveable," "false." For {gigglumois} L. & S. cf. Hipp. 411. 12; Aristot. "de An." iii. 10. 9 = "ball-and-socket joints."

(7) i.e. "forearm."

Moreover, as any damage done to the horse will involve his rider in extreme peril, the horse also should be clad in armour—frontlet, breastplate, and thigh-pieces; (8) which latter may at the same time serve as cuisses for the mounted man. Beyond all else, the horse's belly, being the most vital and defenceless part, should be protected. It is possible to protect it with the saddle-cloth. The saddle itself should be of such sort and so stitched as to give the rider a firm seat, and yet not gall the horse's back.

(8) Cf. "Cyrop." VI. iv. 1; VII. i. 2.

As regards the limbs in general, both horse and rider may be looked upon as fully armed. The only parts remaining are the shins and feet, which of course protrude beyond the cuisses, but these also may be armed by the addition of gaiters made of leather like that used for making sandals. And thus you will have at once defensive armour for the shins and stockings for the feet.

The above, with the blessing of heaven, will serve for armour of defence. To come to weapons of offence, we recommend the sabre rather than the straight sword, (9) since from the vantage-ground of the horse's position the curved blade will descend with greater force than the ordinary weapon.

(9) The {makhaira} (or {kopis}), Persian fashion, rather than the {xephos}. "Cyrop." I. ii. 13.

Again, in place of the long reed spear, which is apt to be weak and awkward to carry, we would substitute two darts of cornel-wood; (10) the one of which the skilful horseman can let fly, and still ply the one reserved in all directions, forwards, backwards, (11) and obliquely; add to that, these smaller weapons are not only stronger than the spear but far more manageable.

(10) For these reforms, the result of the author's Asiatic experiences perhaps, cf. "Hell." III. iv. 14; "Anab." I. viii. 3; "Cyrop." I. ii. 9.

(11) Reading {eis toupisthen} after Leoncl.

As regards range of discharge in shooting we are in favour of the longest possible, as giving more time to rally (12) and transfer the second javelin to the right hand. And here we will state shortly the most effective method of hurling the javelin. The horseman should throw forward his left side, while drawing back his right; then rising bodily from the thighs, he should let fly the missile with the point slightly upwards. The dart so discharged will carry with the greatest force and to the farthest distance; we may add, too, with the truest aim, if at the moment of discharge the lance be directed steadily on the object aimed at. (13)

(12) Al. "to turn right-about."

(13) "If the lance is steadily eyeing the mark at the instant of discharge."

This treatise, consisting of notes and suggestions, lessons and exercises suited to a private individual, must come to a conclusion; the theory and practice of the matter suited to a cavalry commander will be found developed in the companion treatise. (14)

(14) In reference to "The Cavalry General", or "Hipparch."